Happy 1st Thanksgiving!
as a "new" teacher.
I'm thankful we're friends!! :)

Love, Connie   Nov. 2004

Sometimes its Turkey, Sometimes its Feathers

By Lorna & Lecia Balian

Star Bright Books
New York

Published in the United States of America by Star Bright Books, Inc., New York.
The name Star Bright Books and the Star Bright Books logo are registered
trademarks of Star Bright Books, Inc. Please visit www.starbrightbooks.com.

ISBN 1-932065-33-4

Printed in China
9   8   7   6   5   4   3   2   1

Library of Congress Cataloguing-in-Publication Data is available.

For Blanche "Na" Eisenacher
who talks with the animals

Little old Mrs. Gumm found an egg.

She was hunting for wild mushrooms,
and there on the ground,
nearly hidden in a messy nest of leaves,
was a large cream-colored egg —
with freckles.

Yes, indeed!
An egg with freckles.
"Imagine!"

She filled her mushroom basket
with soft new April grass,
placed the egg gently in the center,
and hurried home with her treasure.

Mrs. Gumm was so excited she
almost stepped on Cat,
who was sleeping on the steps.

"Wake up, Cat," she said.
"Wake up and look at our
Thanksgiving dinner!
An egg, Cat. A freckled egg!
A genuine turkey egg, I do believe!"

"We'll try to hatch it, Cat,"
she said, covering the egg
with a soft piece of flannel
and setting it in a warm place.

"We'll hatch it and feed it
and let it grow plump.
What a fine Thanksgiving
dinner we will have.
Imagine."

For days and days
they watched it.
Watched it and
turned it and
warmed it, until
finally, one day in
May they heard a
"tap. . .tap. . .tap."
And there on the
freckled shell was a
tiny crack.

MAY

"Tap. . .tap. . .tap. . . tap, tap, tap."

And the crack became a tiny hole.
They watched and listened,
listened and watched. . .

"It's hatching, Cat," said Mrs. Gumm.
"Oh! What a fine Thanksgiving dinner
we will have."

It was a sticky, wet, boney
little lump that tumbled out
of the cracked, freckled shell.
As it dried it became a fuzzy
little lump with beady black
eyes and a sharp beak.

"He's hungry, Cat," said Mrs. Gumm.
"We'll feed him some oatmeal and fatten him up.
What a fine Thanksgiving dinner we will have.
Imagine!"

Did that turkey eat!
He ate everything in sight!
Oatmeal,
Wheaties,
cornmeal and bread,
seeds,
nuts,
insects,
sand,
and cat food.

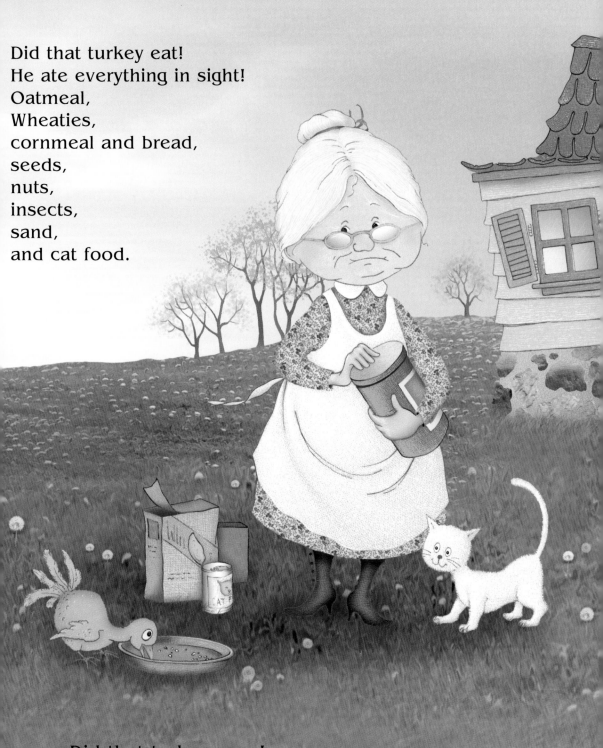

Did that turkey grow!
"Turkey's growing fast, Cat," said Mrs. Gumm.
"He'll be plenty big for Thanksgiving dinner."

In June, while Mrs. Gumm was planting seeds,
Turkey was eating strawberries.
While Mrs. Gumm was looking for strawberries,
Turkey was eating as many seeds as he could find.

"Never mind, Cat," said Mrs. Gumm.
"The more he eats, the plumper he gets,
and what a fine Thanksgiving dinner we will have.
Imagine!"

Turkey ate raspberries in July.
Red raspberries, black raspberries,
white, unripe raspberries —
green peas, inchworms, grass seeds
— and cat food.

"Tsk, tsk, Cat," said Mrs. Gumm.
"Raspberry jam would have been tasty
with our Thanksgiving dinner,
but at least there will be plenty of turkey."

The grapes grew sweet and purple in August,
and Turkey ate them —
grapes, lima beans, caterpillars, pea gravel —
and cat food.

   "There will be no grape jelly
   this year, Cat," said Mrs. Gumm,
   "but what a big, plump Thanksgiving
   turkey we will have. Imagine!"

The September wind blew the thorn apples off the tree,
and Turkey gobbled them up as fast as they fell.
Thorn apples, weed seeds, grasshoppers, ladybugs —
and cat food.

"My, my," said Mrs. Gumm.
"Have you ever seen a plumper bird than that, Cat?
What a fine Thanksgiving dinner we will have."

Mrs. Gumm shelled corn in October.
Turkey helped and Cat watched.

"The corn will make him tasty and tender, Cat.
My, what a delicious Thanksgiving dinner we will have."

Preparations for Thanksgiving Day
began early in November.
Mrs. Gumm found the hatchet —
and ground some corn for cornbread.
She sharpened the hatchet —
and cooked cranberry sauce.
She honed the hatchet —
and baked pumpkin pie.
She polished the hatchet —
and mixed up an onion and chestnut stuffing.

She picked up
the sharp, honed,
polished hatchet and
said,"Wait here, Cat.
It's time to prepare
that big, fat Turkey.
What a fine
Thanksgiving dinner
we will have!"

What a feast!
Cornbread, all warm and crumbly.
Bright red, sticky sweet cranberry sauce.
Spicy, golden pumpkin pie.
A steaming bowl of fragrant onion and
chestnut stuffing — and cat food.

"Sit right down, Cat,"
said Mrs. Gumm.
"I'll bring that nice plump
Turkey to the table. What a
fine Thanksgiving this will be!"

"I have so much to be thankful for,"
said Mrs. Gumm. "A Thanksgiving feast,
and two good friends to share it with.
Imagine!"

"He'll be bigger — and much plumper —
next Thanksgiving," said little old Mrs. Gumm.
"IMAGINE!"